Peter Rabbit's

Little Book of
Harmony

FREDERICK WARNE
Published by the Penguin Group
Penguin Books Ltd, 27 Wrights Lane, London W8 5TZ, England
Penguin Putnam Inc., 375 Hudson Street, New York, NY 10014, USA
Penguin Books Australia Ltd, Ringwood, Victoria, Australia
Penguin Books Canada Ltd, 10 Alcorn Avenue, Toronto, Ontario, Canada M4V 3B2
Penguin Books (N.Z.) Ltd, Private Bag 102902, NSMC, Auckland, New Zealand
Penguin Books India (P) Ltd, 11 Community Centre, Panchsheel Park, New Delhi 110 017, India
Penguin Books (South Africa) (Pty) Ltd, 5 Watkins Street, Denver Ext 4, 2094, South Africa

Penguin Books Ltd, Registered Offices: Harmondsworth, Middlesex, England

First published by Frederick Warne 2000
This edition first published 2000

1 3 5 7 9 10 8 6 4 2

ISBN 0 7232 4642 4

Printed in Hong Kong by Wing King Tong Co. Ltd

One table-spoonful to
be taken at bedtime.

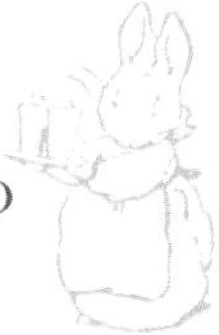

Beatrix Potter led a rather solitary childhood, typical for a girl of her class living in the Victorian era. Time spent with her parents was infrequent and she was not permitted to have friends of her own age. Instead, she had her many and varied pets for company, whom she studied avidly. It is hardly surprising that she when she came to write her Tales, she created an imaginary world inhabited by animals rather than people.

But in as much as her Tales are escapist, they are also laced with reality and diversity, so much of which has a pertinent application to our own motley existence.

The world of Beatrix Potter is not syrupy or banal; she embraces harmony, devotion and respect but occasionally gives a wry smile to rivalry and antagonism. Above all, Beatrix Potter recognises that it takes all sorts to make a world.

Peter Rabbit:
Family Strife

Flopsy, Mopsy and Cotton-tail, who were good little bunnies, went down the lane to gather blackberries. But Peter, who was very naughty, ran straight away to Mr. McGregor's garden and squeezed under the gate.

The Tale of Peter Rabbit

The ambivalence of sibling relationships is commonplace. As children discover who they are, they compete to find their own niche – their differing talents, activities and interests are a way of establishing separate identities, whether it be picking fruit for the family or trespassing on private property.

. . . they did not awake because
the lettuces had been so soporific.
The Flopsy Bunnies dreamt that their
mother was turning them over in bed.

The Tale of The Flopsy Bunnies

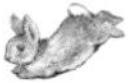

Dream interpretation is a complex and personal endeavour. But generally speaking, dreaming about your mother may symbolize a variety of feelings and ideas – caring, nurturing, love, hard work, sacrifice, martyrdom . . . Dreaming about rabbits represents luck, quickness, fertility, pregnancy, and magic. However, we are unsure about whether the same applies if one is, indeed, a rabbit.

Alexander went into squeals of laughter. Then he pricked Pigling with the pin that fastened his pig paper; and when Pigling slapped him he dropped the pin, and tried to take Pigling's pin . . .

The Tale of Pigling Bland

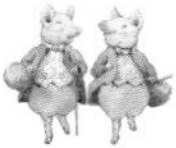

Sometimes siblings fight with each other because they are stressed about other things. Sending your children 'off to market', for example, constitutes a major transition and may bring out the beast in them. Try not to intervene in arguments unless they turn violent – the use of sharp implements such as pins, for example, should be your cue to step in.

"I'm in sad trouble, Cousin Ribby . . .

I've lost my dear son Thomas, I'm afraid the
rats have got him." She wiped her eyes with her apron.

"He's a bad kitten, Cousin Tabitha; he made a cat's
cradle of my best bonnet last time I came to tea . . .
I will help you to find him; and whip him too! . . ."

The Tale of Samuel Whiskers

Always say nice things about someone else's child,
even if the child is a frightful delinquent. Back seat
drivers and busybodies rank very highly in terms of
unpopular members of society.

When Flopsy and Benjamin came back—
old Mr. Bouncer woke up. Tommy Brock and all
the young rabbit-babies had disappeared!
Mr. Bouncer would not confess that he had admitted
anybody into the rabbit-hole. But the smell of
badger was undeniable . . . He was in disgrace;
Flopsy wrung her ears, and slapped him.

The Tale of Mr. Tod

The extended family! Live-in grandparents can be
handy as babysitters, but terribly frustrating when
they 'lend' your babies to the local fiend. Slapping
the elderly is, of course, monstrous. Hiding their
favourite pipe and slippers is suitably humane.

At this point, old Mrs. Rabbit's voice was heard inside the rabbit-hole, calling—"Cotton-tail! Cotton-tail! Fetch some more camomile!" Peter said he thought he might feel better if he went for a walk.

The Tale of Benjamin Bunny

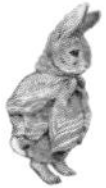

Daughters often feel the injustice of being tied up with domestic duties while their wayward brothers casually swagger out of the burrow without a by-your-leave. Make him do the housework now or you will have his future wife to answer to.

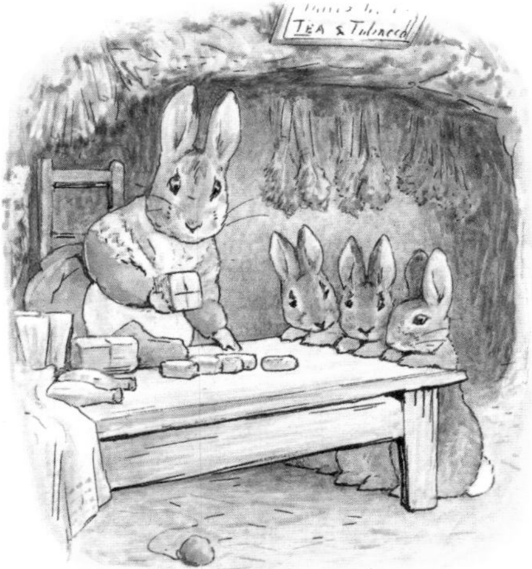
TEA & Tobacco

Her sister-in-law, Mrs. Rebbecah Puddle-duck,
was perfectly willing to leave the hatching to
someone else—"I have not the patience to sit on a nest
for twenty-eight days; and no more have you, Jemima.
You would let them go cold; you know you would!"

The Tale of Jemima Puddle-Duck

Insufferable, inconsiderate, inconvenient – in-laws.
As if our siblings hadn't caused enough trouble
during childhood, they administer the final insult by
marrying someone awful. Rumour has it that they do
this precisely to make you see how lucky you were
to have them while you were growing up.

"I scarcely like to send him alone, though he
is sensible for his size . . ." Aunt Dorcas and
Aunt Porcas stood in the porch. They watched
him safely out of sight, down the field,
and through the first of many stiles.

The Tale of Little Pig Robinson

When children leave home for the first time, many
parents experience feelings of anxiety and loss, known
informally as the Empty Nest Syndrome. Other parents,
however, wave goodbye with a wry smile on their face as
they reminisce over the phone bill, wet towels on the
floor, insufferable music, slamming doors . . . .

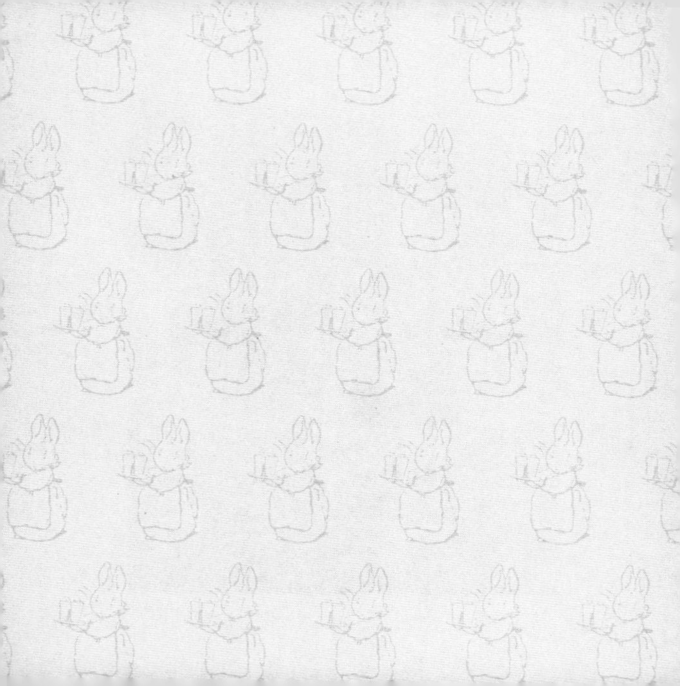

Pigling Bland:
A Fine Romance

A perfectly lovely little black Berkshire pig stood smiling beside him. She had twinkly little screwed up eyes, a double chin, and a short turned up nose. She pointed at Pigling's plate; he hastily gave it to her, and fled to the meal chest.

The Tale of Pigling Bland

Love at First Sight is an intoxicating series of highs and lows, triggered by intense physical attraction. Be wary of allowing your feelings to overwhelm you before you develop adequate emotional intimacy. On the other hand – carpe diem! – it certainly worked for Pigling Bland.

Now who is this knocking at Cotton-tail's door?
Tap tappit! Tap tappit! She's heard it before?
And when she peeps out there is nobody there,
but a present of carrots put down on the stair.

Appley Dapply's Nursery Rhymes

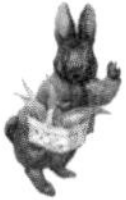

During the wooing process, it is wise to present the object of your desire with meaningful gifts. While a basket of carrots says 'true love' to a rabbit, it may be more appropriate for the average suitor to say it with flowers.

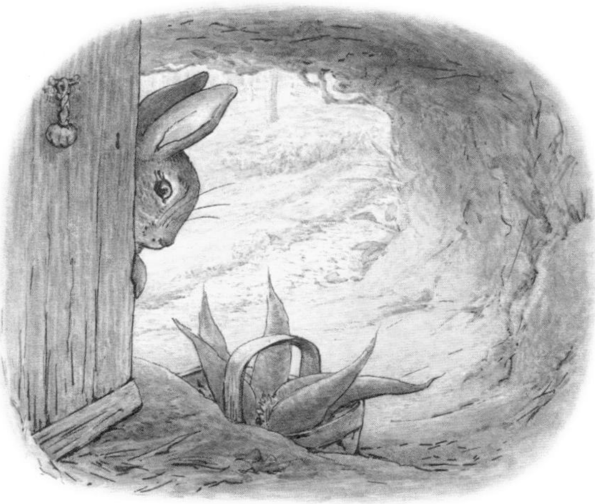

Cecily Parsley lived in a pen,
and brewed good ale for gentlemen;
Gentlemen came every day,
till Cecily Parsley ran away.
Cecily Parsley's Nursery Rhymes

Gentlemen and ale — a lethal combination.
Setting yourself up as a licensed vendor of liquor
can be a tricky business. For although you are
likely to attract a vast number of thirsty admirers,
you are also likely to encounter 'Ale Humour'.
Follow Cecily's fine example.

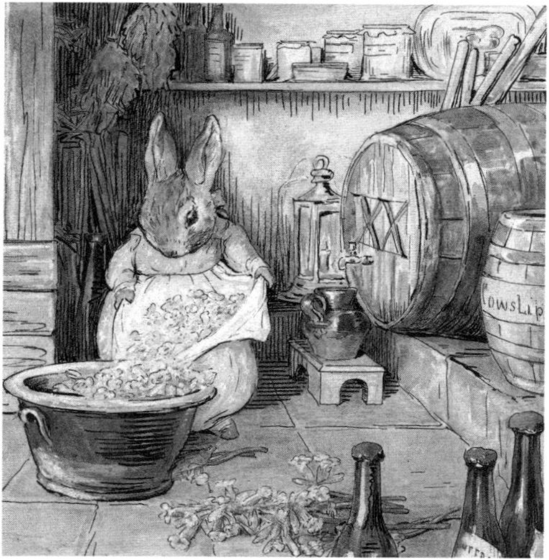
XX
CowsLip

The water was all slippy-sloppy in the larder and in the back passage. But Mr. Jeremy Fisher liked getting his feet wet; nobody ever scolded him, and he never caught a cold!

The Tale of Mr. Jeremy Fisher

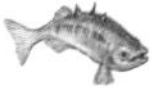

The infamous bachelor pad may be scrupulously clean or astonishingly squalid, but it is always scented with the rather overpowering 'Fear of The Big Commitment'. Should you find yourself attracted to the proprietor, remember these fine words: Love may turn frogs into princes, but marriage turns them quietly back.

Goody Tiptoes:
Marital Bliss

Goody Tiptoes passed a lonely and unhappy night . . .
In the meantime Timmy Tiptoes came to his senses . . .
"But how shall I ever get out? My wife will be anxious!"
"Just another nut—or two nuts; let me crack
them for you," said the Chipmunk.

The Tale of Timmy Tiptoes

Led astray by an indelicate acquaintance, the errant
husband soon finds himself unable to move and in dire
need of home comforts. Acceptance back into the
homestead is dependent on levels of tolerance and
frequency of desertion.

"Line your old cloak?" shouted Mr. McGregor—
"I shall sell them and buy myself baccy!" "Rabbit tobacco!
I shall skin them and cut off their heads." Mrs. McGregor
untied the sack and put her hand inside. When she felt
the vegetables she became very very angry. She said that
Mr. McGregor had "done it a purpose."

The Tale of The Flopsy Bunnies

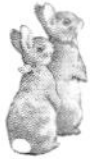

One of the most important things to remember during a marital dispute is to employ melodrama and archaic syntax, adding potency to your fight and an element of charm to an otherwise humdrum quarrel.

There was a pattering noise and an old woman rat poked her head round a rafter. All in a minute she rushed upon Tom Kitten, and before he knew what was happening—

His coat was pulled off, and he was rolled up in a bundle, and tied with string in very hard knots. . .

The old rat watched her and took snuff.

The Tale of Samuel Whiskers

Take note: behind every great rat there is a great woman rat. It has even been suggested that women are physically, as well as mentally, stronger than men and that denial of this reality is not a means of massaging the male ego but of avoiding drear manual activities.

. . . they began to empty the bags into a hole high up in a tree, that had belonged to a woodpecker; the nuts rattled down—down—down inside. "How shall you ever get them out again? It is like a money-box!" said Goody. "I shall be much thinner before spring-time, my love," said Timmy Tiptoes, peeping into the hole.

The Tale of Timmy Tiptoes

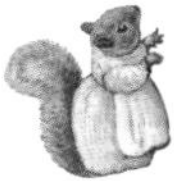

Promises, promises.

Johnny Town-Mouse: Between Friends

"I am sure you will never want to live in town again," said Timmy Willie. But he did. He went back in the very next hamper of vegetables, he said it was too quiet!!

The Tale of Johnny Town-Mouse

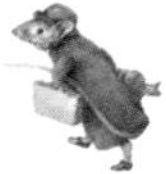

True friendships are never ended by minor matters such as physical separation, preference for serenity or noise, or even whether one's taste in footwear runs to Country Bumpkin rubber wellies or City Slicker leather brogues. If one insists on only being friends with people just like oneself, one may find that one ends up with no friends at all.

". . . Oh I do wish I could eat my own pie, instead of a pie made of mouse!" Duchess considered and considered . . . "Oh what a good idea! Why shouldn't I rush along and put my pie into Ribby's oven when Ribby isn't there?"

The Tale of The Pie and The Patty Pan

Many an unpleasant pie has been eaten for the sake of etiquette and many a friendship harmed by covert scheming. Be assured that no one gained a place in high society without regular indigestible luncheons. A life of harmony is a constant trade-off between behaving as you wish and offending your friends.

"Madam, have you lost your way?" said he . . . Jemima thought him mighty civil and handsome. She explained that she had not lost her way, but that she was trying to find a convenient dry nesting-place.

The Tale of Jemima Puddle-Duck

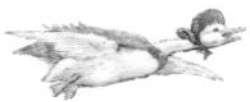

Jemima regards the gentleman's refinement and pleasing semblance as a measure of his worth as a friend. Of course, Jemima is not noted for her perception or wisdom. The ability to charm the birds from the trees is a dishonourable quality. Don't be a Jemima.

But Simpkin set down the pipkin of milk upon the dresser, and looked suspiciously at the tea-cups. He wanted his supper of little fat mouse! "Simpkin," said the tailor, "where is my TWIST?" But Simpkin hid a little parcel privately in the teapot, and spit and growled at the tailor. . .

The Tailor of Gloucester

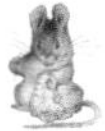

True friendship is totally without self-interest. Expecting payment for good deeds is an absurd oversight since enduring companionship is a far richer reward than a little fat mouse (and considerably more palatable). Cats, of course, make their own rules.

Peter did not seem to be enjoying himself;
he kept hearing noises. Benjamin, on the contrary,
was perfectly at home, and ate a lettuce leaf.

The Tale of Benjamin Bunny

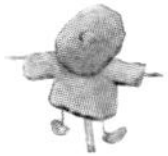

If you will allow yourself to be led astray by adventurous friends, you might as well enjoy the experience. While Peter grapples with his nerves, Benjamin Bunny's nonchalant manner makes for a far more agreeable outing. Take note: crunching noisily on a lettuce leaf is an excellent way of drowning out the voice of your conscience.

Hunca Munca:
Love Thy Neighbour

Then those mice set to work to do all the mischief they could—especially Tom Thumb! He took Jane's clothes out of the chest of drawers in her bedroom, and he threw them out of the top floor window.

The Tale of Two Bad Mice

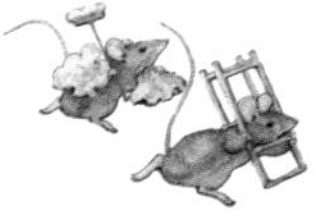

Annoying neighbours can be galling until one considers that 'disruptive' is a comparative term. Always ensure that you are more of a nuisance to your neighbours than they are to you.

Presently the rats came back and set to work to make him into a dumpling. First they smeared him with butter, and then they rolled him in the dough.

The Tale of Samuel Whiskers

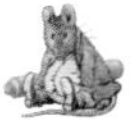

Partners in crime make superlative companions and the rodent world's answer to Bonnie and Clyde are no exception. Two people who possess enough information to have one another severely castigated have forged a relationship in which mutual trust and co-dependence are assured.

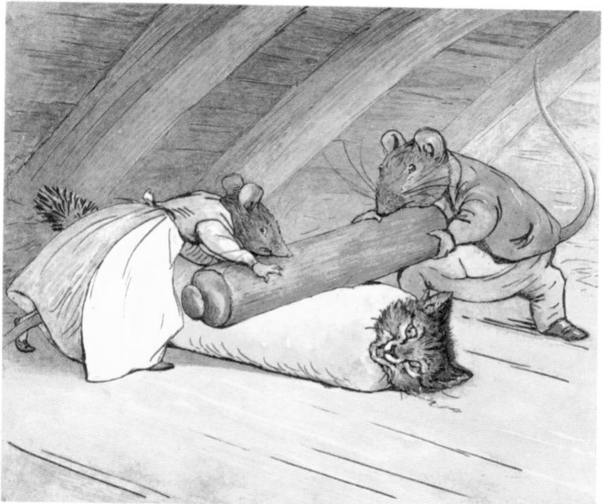

He sat and smiled, and the water dripped off his coat-tails. Mrs. Tittlemouse went round with a mop. He sat such a while that he had to be asked if he would take some dinner? . . . Mr. Jackson rose ponderously from the table, and began to look into the cupboards.

The Tale of Mrs. Tittlemouse

Putting down roots in your neighbour's abode is an exceptional way of driving them to distraction. Listen out for that grudging offer of refreshment — it is a cue to leave, not an invitation to snoop in their pantry.

Ginger and Pickles: Nine to Five

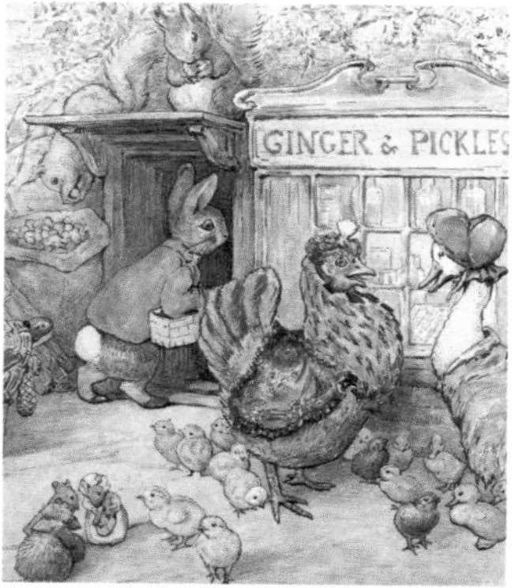
GINGER & PICKLES

The shop was also patronised by mice—only the mice were rather afraid of Ginger. Ginger usually requested Pickles to serve them, because he said it made his mouth water. "I cannot bear," said he, "to see them going out at the door carrying their little parcels." "I have the same feeling about rats," replied Pickles, "but it would never do to eat our customers . . ."

The Tale of Ginger and Pickles

First rule of business: the customer is not necessarily always right, but they must at least be permitted to shop without fear of being devoured.

Old Mr. Brown turned up his eyes in disgust at the impertinence of Nutkin. But he ate up the honey! The squirrels filled their little sacks with nuts. But Nutkin sat upon a big flat rock, and played ninepins with a crab apple and green fir-cones.

The Tale of Squirrel Nutkin

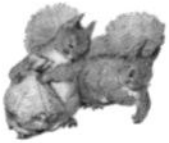

Squirrel Nutkin's work ethic reads quite clearly: hard work never killed anybody, but why take chances? Of course, one must not exist for the sake of making a living, but skittles certainly won't pay the bills.

And Miss Dormouse refused to take back the ends
when they were brought back to her with complaints.
And when Mr. John Dormouse was complained to,
he stayed in bed, and would say nothing but "very snug";
which is not a sound way to carry on a retail business.

The Tale of Ginger and Pickles

For those who are particularly prone to impromptu bouts
of shut-eye, running a business is highly inappropriate.
A leisurely trip to the Land of Nod will always triumph –
hard work has a future, but laziness pays off immediately.

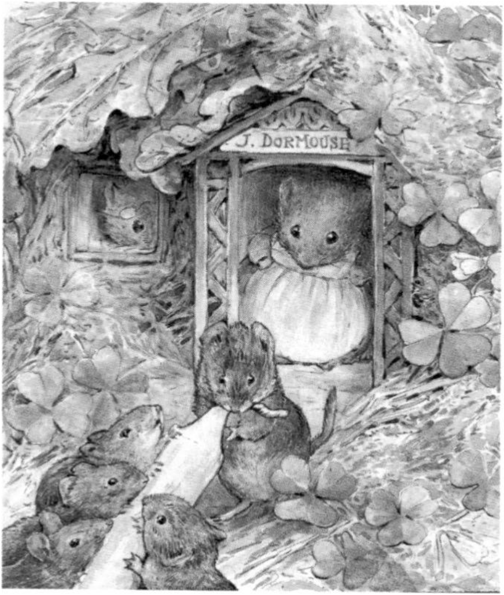
J. DORMOUSE

Such a shop! Such a jumble! Wool all sorts of colours, thick wool, thin wool, fingering wool, and rug wool, bundles and bundles all jumbled up; and she could not put her hoof on anything. She was so confused and slow at finding things that Betsy got impatient.

The Tale of Little Pig Robinson

Practice the ancient art of Feng Shui in the workplace in order to harness positive energies. Reduce clutter in order to encourage harmony and thwart woolly thinking – even organised chaos is bad for the soul.